Kingston Libraries

Cr ıy

Crabtree Publishing Company
www.crabtreebooks.com
1-800-387-7650

PMB 59051, 350 Fifth Ave.
59th Floor,
New York, NY 10118

616 Welland Ave.
St. Catharines, ON
L2M 5V6

Published by Crabtree Publishing in 2013
Printed in Hong Kong/012013/BK20121102

Series editor: Melanie Palmer
Editor: Kathy Middleton
Notes for adults: Reagan Miller
Series advisors: Dr. Hilary Minns, Catherine Glavina
Series designer: Peter Scoulding
**Production coordinator and
   Prepress technician:** Margaret Amy Salter
Print coordinator: Katherine Berti

Text (Ride, Ride, Ride Your Bike)
© Wes Magee 2010
Illustration © Marina Le Ray 2010

First published in 2010
by Franklin Watts
(A division of Hachette
Children's Books)

**Library and Archives Canada
Cataloguing in Publication**

Magee, Wes, 1939-
       Row, row, row your boat ; and, Ride, ride,
ride your bike / retold by Wes Magee ; illus[...]
by Marina Le Ray.

(Tadpoles: nursery rhymes)
Issued also in electronic format.
ISBN 978-0-7787-1149-0 (bound).--ISBN 978-[...]
7787-1153-7 (pbk.)

       1. Nursery rhymes, English. I. Le Ray,
Marina II. Title. III. Title: Ride, ride, ride yo[...]
bike. IV. Series: Tadpoles (St. Catharines, On[...]
Nursery rhymes

PZ8.3.M34Ro 2013   j398.8   C2012-907[...]

**Library of Congress
Cataloging-in-Publication Data**

Magee, Wes, 1939-
       [Poetry. Selections]

2012043747

Row, Row, Row Your Boat

Marina Le Ray

"I like the idea of rowing a boat down a stream on a lovely, sunny day, and all the wildlife you would see along the way."

Row, row, row your boat

5

gently down
the stream.

7

Merrily, merrily,

8

merrily, merrily,

life is but a dream.

11

Row, Row, Row Your Boat

Row, row, row your boat

gently down the stream.

Merrily, merrily,

merrily, merrily,

life is but a dream.

Can you point to the rhyming words?

Ride, Ride, Ride Your Bike

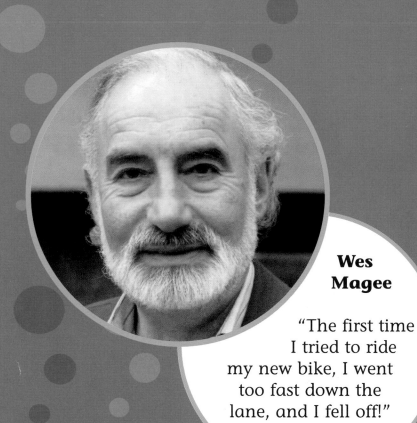

Wes Magee

"The first time I tried to ride my new bike, I went too fast down the lane, and I fell off!"

Ride, ride, ride your bike

up the muddy lane.

Bumpity, bumpity,
bumpity, bumpity,

19

ride it back again.

Ride, Ride, Ride Your Bike

Ride, ride, ride your bike

up the muddy lane.

 Bumpity, bumpity,

bumpity, bumpity,

ride it back again.

Can you point to the
rhyming words?

Puzzle Time!

1.

2.

3.

Choose the right action for the picture.

Notes for adults

TADPOLES NURSERY RHYMES are structured for emergent readers. The books may also be used for read-alouds or shared reading with young children.

The language of nursery rhymes is often already familiar to an emergent reader. Seeing the rhymes in print helps build phonemic awareness skills. The alternative rhymes extend and enhance the reading experience further, and encourage children to be creative with language and make up their own rhymes.

IF YOU ARE READING THIS BOOK WITH A CHILD, HERE ARE A FEW SUGGESTIONS:

1. Make reading fun! Choose a time to read when you and the child are relaxed and have time to share the story.

2. Recite the nursery rhyme together before you start reading. What might the alternative rhyme be about? Brainstorm ideas.

3. Encourage the child to reread the rhyme and to retell it using his or her own words. Invite the child to use the illustrations as a guide.

4. Help the child identify the rhyming words when the whole rhymes are repeated on pages 12 and 22. This activity builds phonological awareness and decoding skills. Encourage the child to make up alternative rhymes.

5. Give praise! Children learn best in a positive environment.

IF YOU ENJOYED THIS BOOK, WHY NOT TRY ANOTHER TITLE FROM TADPOLES: NURSERY RHYMES?

VISIT WWW.CRABTREEBOOKS.COM FOR OTHER CRABTREE BOOKS.

Answer
The correct action is picture 3.

24